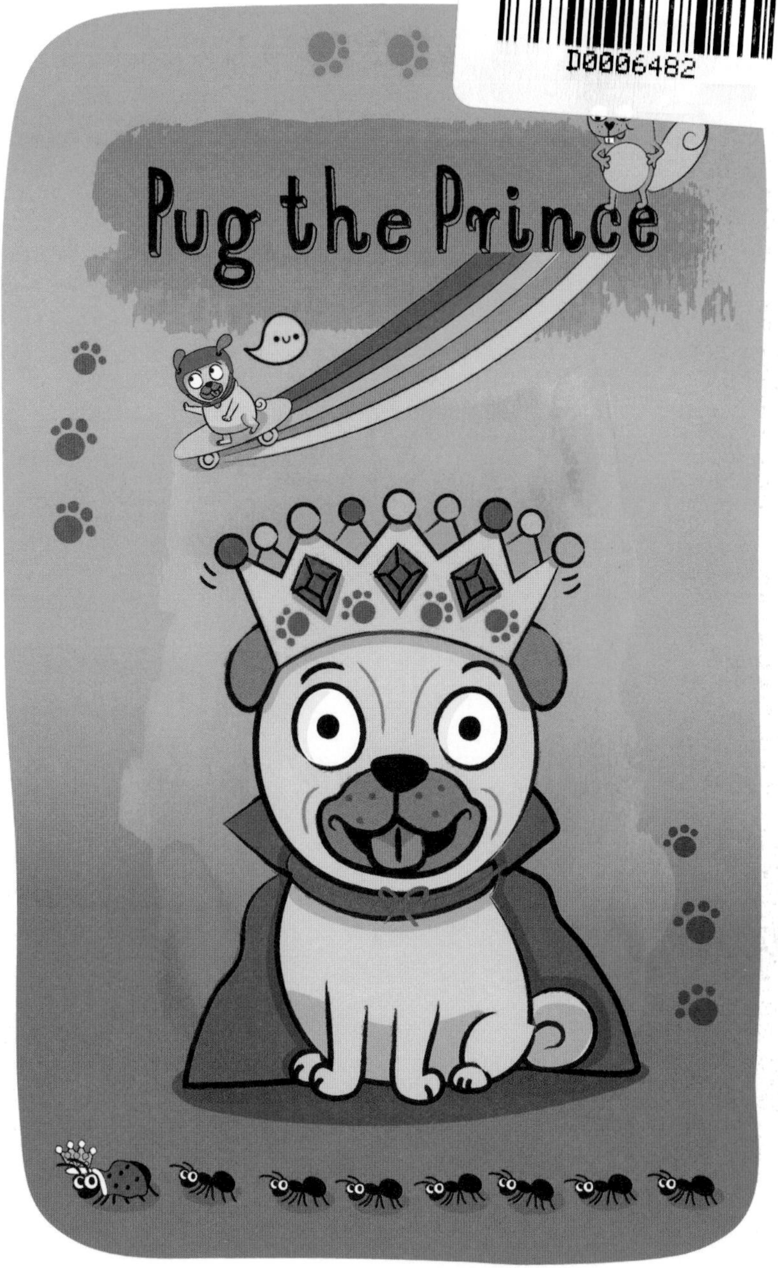
Pug the Prince

Read all the Diary of a Pug books!

More books coming soon!

DIARY OF A PUG

Pug the Prince

By *Kyla May*

SCHOLASTIC INC.

To my amazing daughter Jaida,
who never had a book named after her.

Special thanks to Madelyn Rosenberg

Art copyright © 2023 by Kyla May
Text copyright © 2023 by Scholastic Inc.

Photos © KylaMay2019

Library of Congress Cataloging-in-Publication Data
Names: May, Kyla, author, illustrator.
Title: Pug the prince / by Kyla May.
Description: First edition. I New York, NY : Branches/Scholastic Inc., 2023. I Series: Diary of a pug ; Book 9 I I Summary: When Bella wins a poster-making contest at the animal shelter, she gets to be queen of the "Adopt-an-Animal"; parade. That can only mean one thing . . . Bub the pug is her prince! But Bub has no idea what a prince does. Can he figure it out in time to help Bella be the best queen she can be?
Identifiers: LCCN 2022034327 (print) I ISBN9781338877588 (reinforced library binding) I ISBN 9781338877571 (paperback)
Subjects: CYAC: Pug—Fiction. I Dogs—Fiction. I Parades—Fiction. I Human-animal relationships—Fiction. I LCGFT: Humorous fiction.
Classification: LCC PZ7.M4535 Pv 2023 (print) I DDC [Fic]—dc23
LC record available at https://lccn.loc.gov/2022034327

978-1-338-87757-1 (paperback) / 978-1-338-87758-8 (reinforced library binding)

10 9 8 7 6 5 4 3 2 1   23 24 25 26 27

Printed in China   62
First edition, October 2023
Edited by AnnMarie Anderson
Book design by Kyla May and Christian Zelaya

Table of Contents

1. A Royal Announcement...............1

2. The Royal Pain.....................9

3. Prince Pug...........................17

4. Royal Wave.........................26

5. Ant-ics...............................37

6. Losing the Crown.................46

7. Fit for a Queen....................55

8. A Royal Celebration...............65

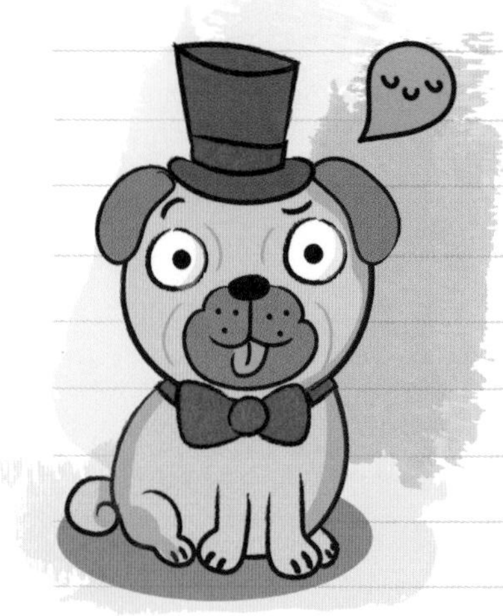

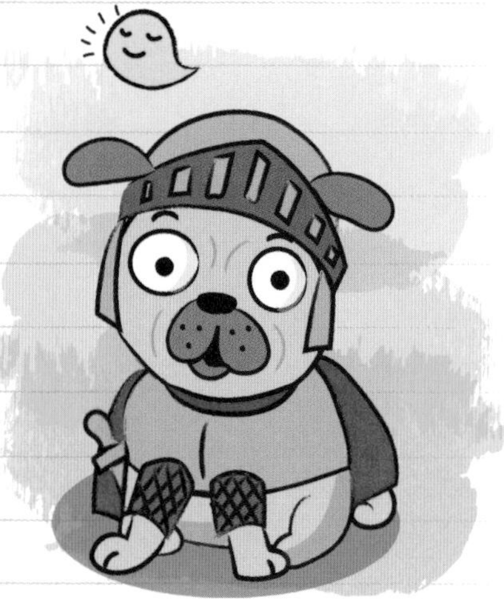

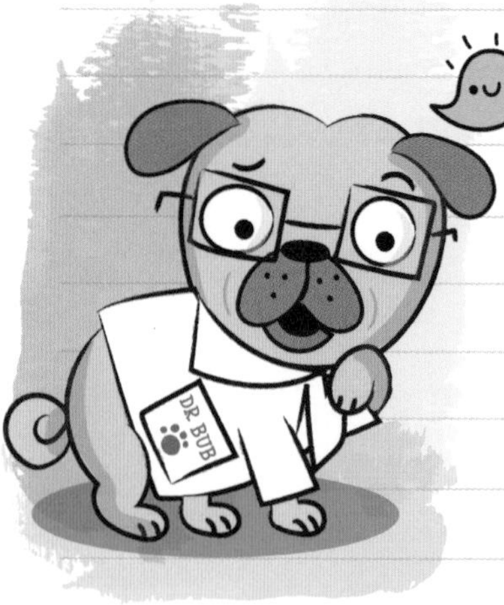
DR. BUB

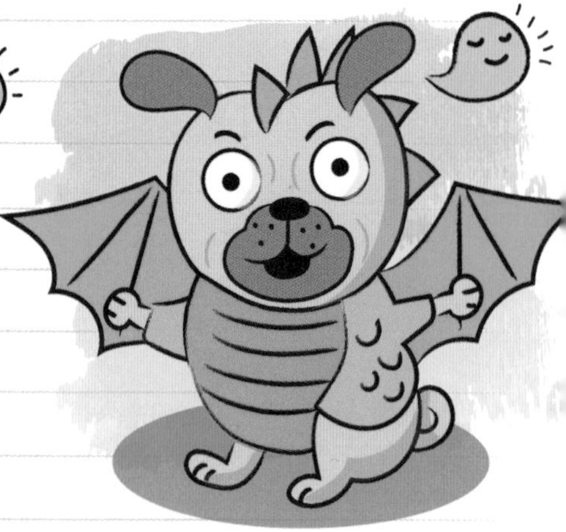

Chapter 1

A ROYAL ANNOUNCEMENT

SATURDAY

Dear Diary,

BUB here, with some big news that really rules! But first, here are some things to know about me.

I am the prince of fashion!

I make many different faces:

Thinking Face

Royal Face

Running Away from the Bathtub Face

Here are some of my favorite things:
PEANUT BUTTER

Hey! That's my favorite, too!

MY BEST FRIENDS, BEAR AND LUNA

MY HUMAN, BELLA

You're the best!

No, YOU are!

Here are some things that are NOT my favorite:

DUCHESS

Step aside. Royalty coming through.

NUTZ

And my least favorite thing of all:

WATER.

That means baths, too. The first bath
I remember is when Bella brought me
home from the pet adoption fair. The tub
was full of bubbles. It looked so fun!

It was NOT fun. That's when Bella gave
me my full name, BARON VON BUBBLES.
But I go by Bub for short.

Okay, here's the big news, Diary. Today, Bella came home with a royal announcement.

Guess what? I won the poster-making contest at the animal shelter! The theme was "Be Kind to Animals."

Hey! Where am I?

KEEP THIS IN
♥ MIND, ♥
ALWAYS BE
KIND.

Diary, I'm so glad Bella won! No one is kinder to animals than her!

As a prize for winning, Bella's poster will hang all over town. That way, people will know about the animals they can adopt from the shelter. And there's something else, too!

I'm going to be queen of the Adopt-an-Animal Parade!

I'm living with real royalty. I wonder how royalty behaves?

QUEEN BELLA

Chapter 2

THE ROYAL PAIN

SUNDAY

Dear Diary,

As queen, Bella will ride on the parade float. She will lead her <u>royal subjects</u>. (That's a fancy name for the animals from the shelter!) And guess what else?

If I'm the queen, you're my prince, Bub!

I'm a prince! Prince Bub!

I was so excited, Diary! But what does a prince do?

I'm sure princes give their friends peanut butter treats.

I can show you a thing or two about being royal! I am a Duchess, after all.

Bella wasn't sure how to be a queen, either.

What do queens DO all day?

We have a lot of reading to do.

Bella is good at everything. I'm sure she'll figure it out. But will I? There's only one week until the big parade.

I asked my friend Luna for help. She lives next door with Bella's friend Jack.

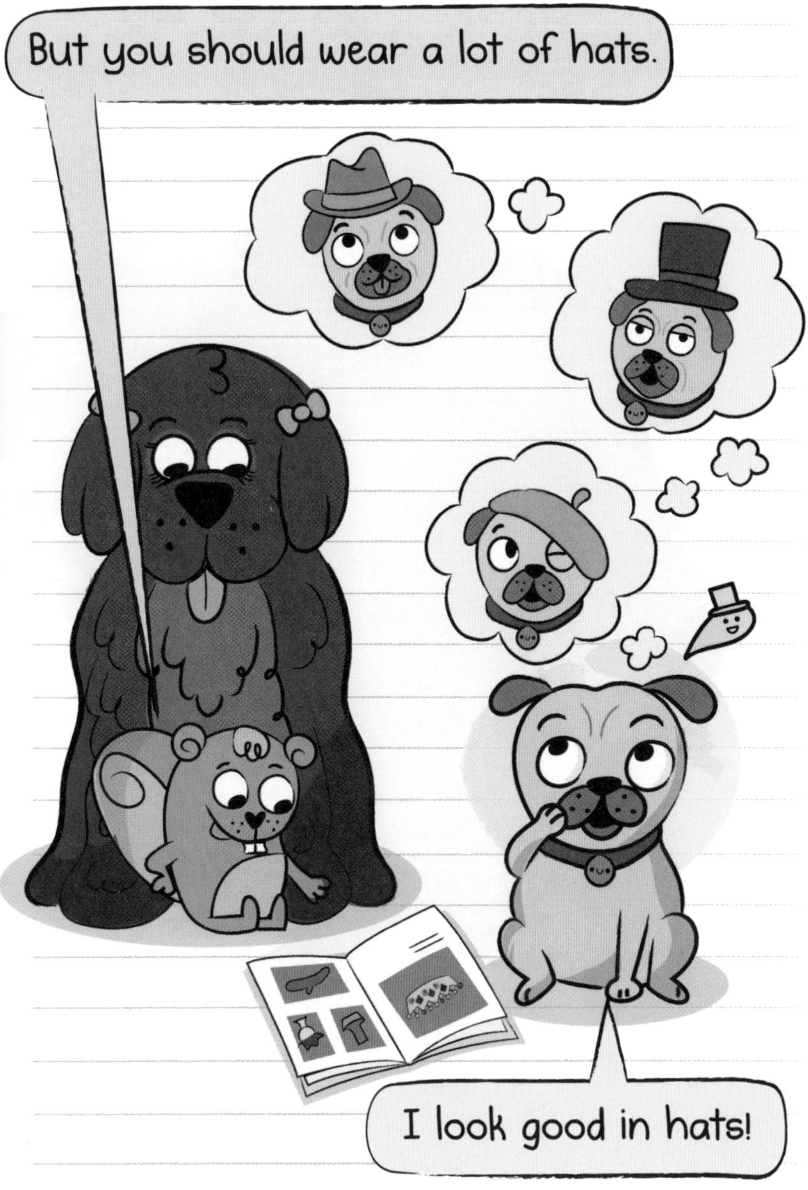
But you should wear a lot of hats.
I look good in hats!

Duchess tried to help, too. She had a lot of rules for me to follow.

Riding a skateboard is NOT royal.

You should drink tea, like the king of England.

Diary, Duchess was being a royal pain.

I was getting nervous. And when I get nervous, I get . . . gassy.

That is NOT royal.

I'm pretty sure princes don't do that. At least not in public.

If being Bella's prince means daily baths, I'm not sure I can handle it. But I'll try, for Bella.

Chapter 3

PRINCE PUG

MONDAY

Dear Diary,

Bella had a lot to learn about being the parade queen. Jack adopted Luna from the shelter, so he wanted to help.

I'll be your royal friend AND royal coach!

Jack, Luna, Bella, and I went to the shelter to learn more.

Did you know a queen has to wave a certain way?

PARADE QUEEN BUILDS FLOAT!

Really? Do queens also hold a hammer a certain way?

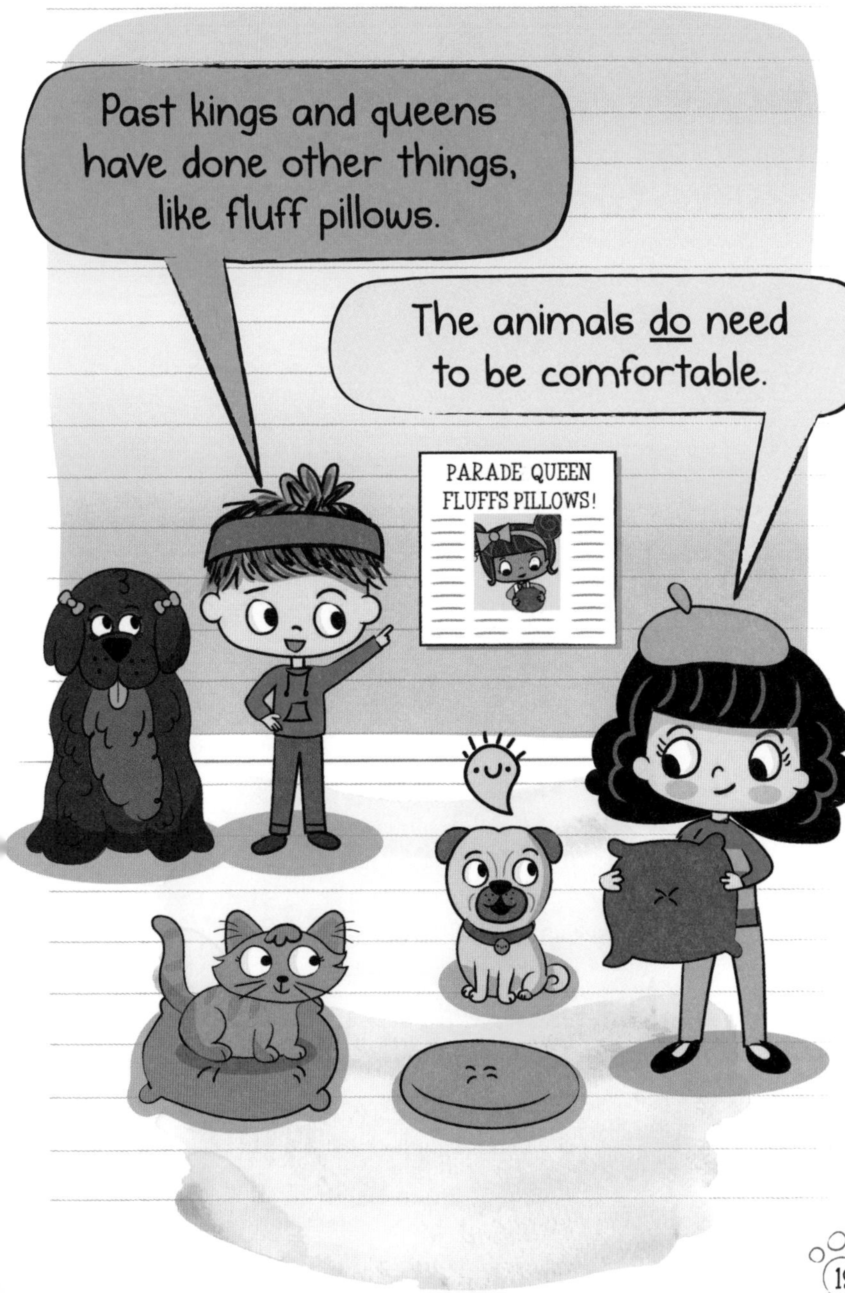
Past kings and queens have done other things, like fluff pillows.
The animals do need to be comfortable.
PARADE QUEEN FLUFFS PILLOWS!

As queen, Bella will have to smile a lot. Her posters will be all over town. Everyone will know about the parade and the adoption fair!

WINNING POSTER

KEEP THIS IN MIND, ALWAYS BE KIND.

Here are your posters!

Thanks!

Jack says last year's queen played the ukulele and wrote a song about animals. She also held a fancy tea for shelter workers.

Can a prince be a taste tester?

Can a royal friend be a taste tester?

Parade kings and queens make speeches.

They also make their own crowns.

Bella says the most important thing about being queen is caring for the royal subjects. The dogs and cats at the shelter are so cute, Diary!

When you care for someone, you want what's best for them.

The parade will show everyone how awesome you all are! As queen, I will help you find homes with families who love you!

Like our home!

Forever homes for all!

Furr-ever!

A worker gave Bella a list of parade-
queen responsibilities to choose from.
Guess what she decided on?

I'll do EVERYTHING! I just have to
figure out where to start!

MAKE CROWN
WRITE SONG
WRITE SPEECH
BUILD FLOAT
FLUFF PILLOWS
LET PEOPLE KNOW
ABOUT PARADE
PLAY WITH ANIMALS
HAVE FUN

Let's start with the crown!

A crown is easy. I can finish
and cross it off my list!

There was so much to do, Diary. Could
we do it all?

Chapter 4

ROYAL WAVE

TUESDAY

Dear Diary,

Bella made a crown for herself. She also made one for me! I think they need more bling, but I can fix that.

Snazzy! Do I get one?

I don't need a crown to feel royal.

When Bella came home from school, she wanted to go back to the animal shelter.

You're going AGAIN?

There's lots to do.

I'll help! For nine jars of peanut butter!

No, thanks. That's way too much!

At the shelter, Bella and Jack helped build the frame for the parade float.

They made paper flowers to decorate the float.

We'll never get these done!

Jack coached Bella on her waving.

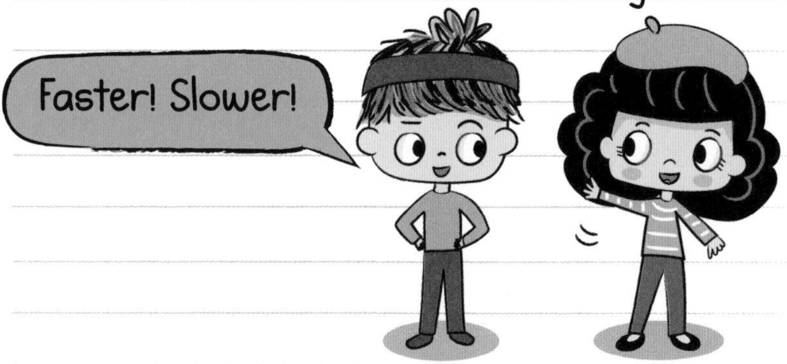
Faster! Slower!

Bella learned to play the ukulele like the last queen.

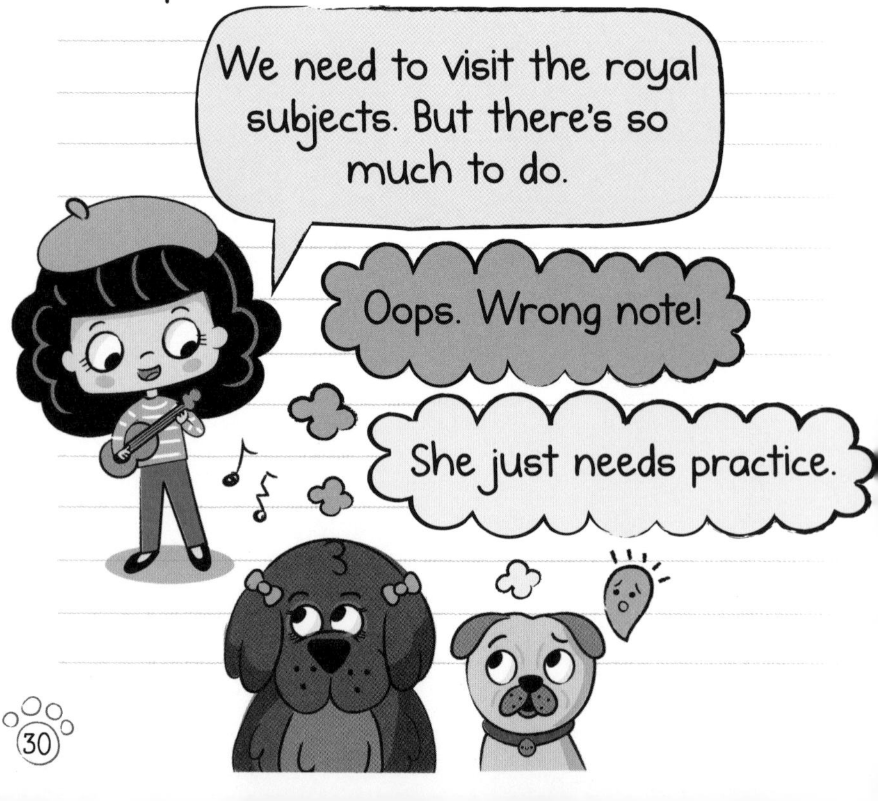
We need to visit the royal subjects. But there's so much to do.
Oops. Wrong note!
She just needs practice.

I had a great idea to help Bella with all
she had to do, Diary.

Let's visit the royal subjects
while Bella is busy.

We'll ask them what
they need most!

The animals still had the toys we donated after we held our pet wash!

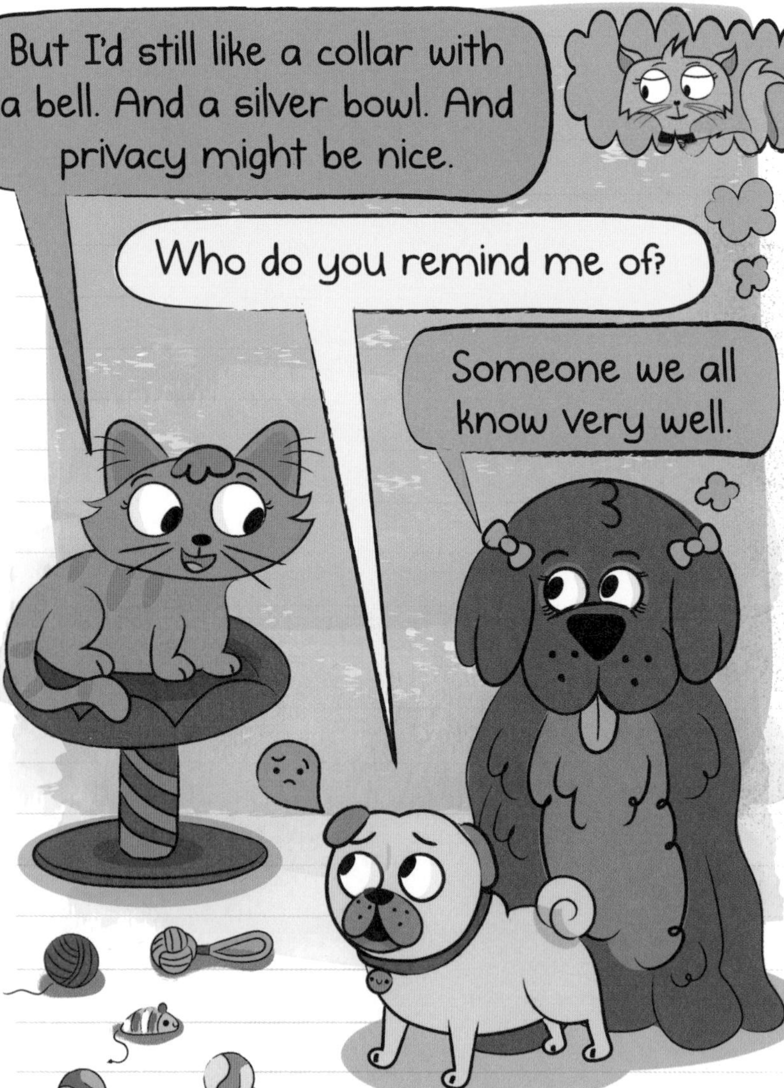

Besides forever homes, the dogs wanted more tennis balls.

What else do you need?

More tennis balls! And hugs.

Bella is a great hugger.

One royal subject looked very sad.

We wanted to cheer him up.

His name was Chester. He was shy but friendly. We had a lot in common.

I'm Prince Bub. How can I help you?

I want a home and hugs. Also, I miss peanut butter treats.

Diary, I hope the parade helps more people see how great the cats and dogs here are. Then they can all find new homes!

We hurried back to Bella.

Looks like the dogs need more tennis balls.

Don't forget the treats!

And hugs and new homes!

I may be a prince, but I'm just one pup. Clearly we needed more help getting things done!

Chapter 5

ANT-ICS

WEDNESDAY

Dear Diary,

I wanted to help Bella's royal subjects. And my royal queen.

You need minions . . . helpers who do whatever you say.

In a palace, the queen has lots of helpers.

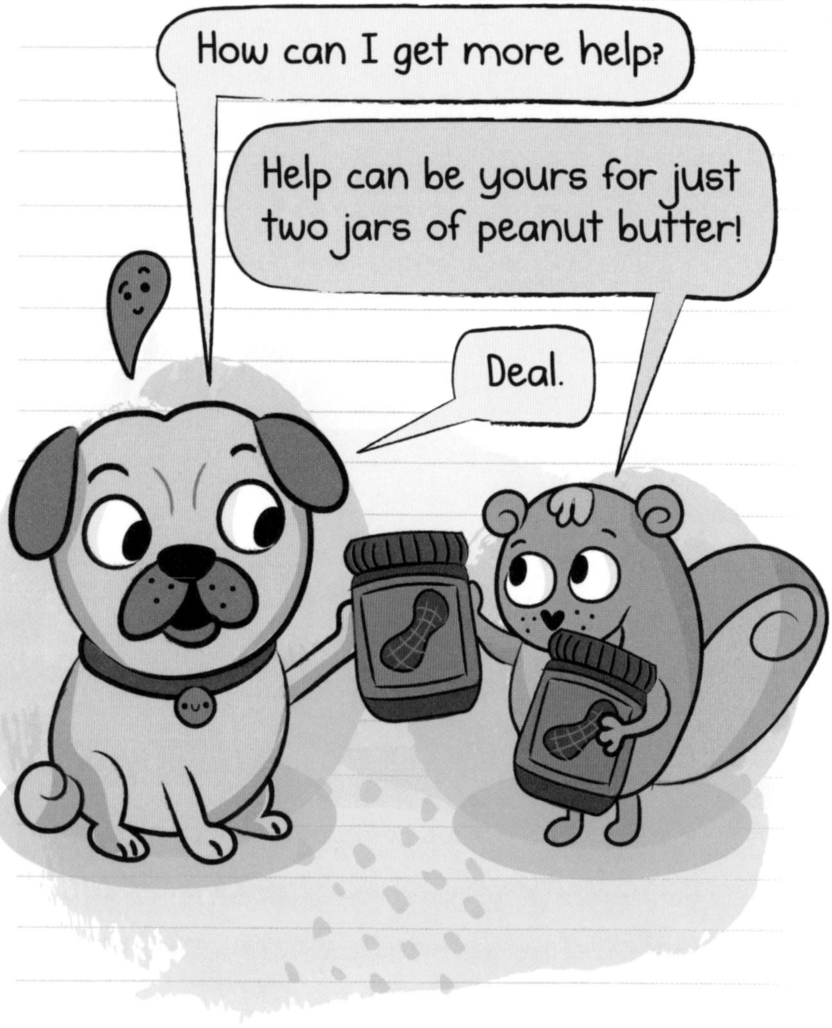
How can I get more help?
Help can be yours for just two jars of peanut butter!
Deal.

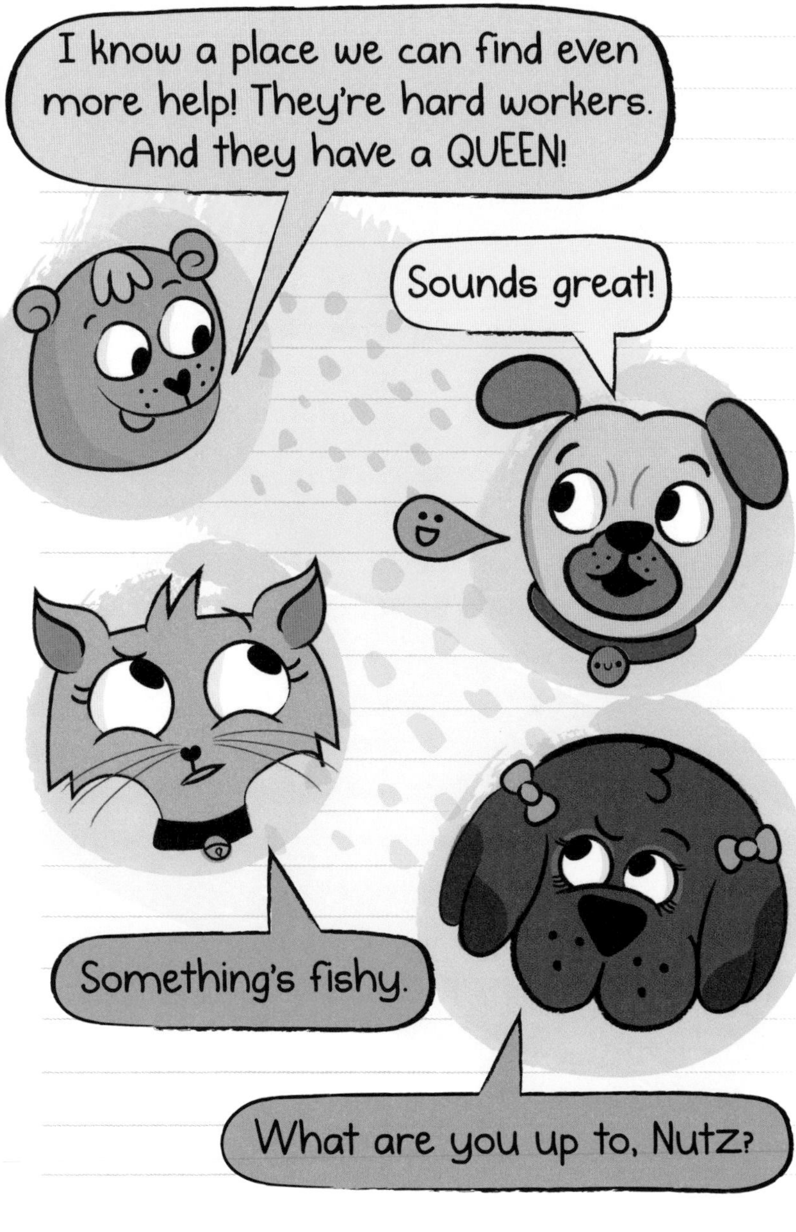
I know a place we can find even more help! They're hard workers. And they have a QUEEN!
Sounds great!
Something's fishy.
What are you up to, Nutz?

Nutz led us across the yard.

The ants were very small. I put my head closer to the ground.

May we speak to your queen, please?

Who's asking?

The ant queen looked very royal.

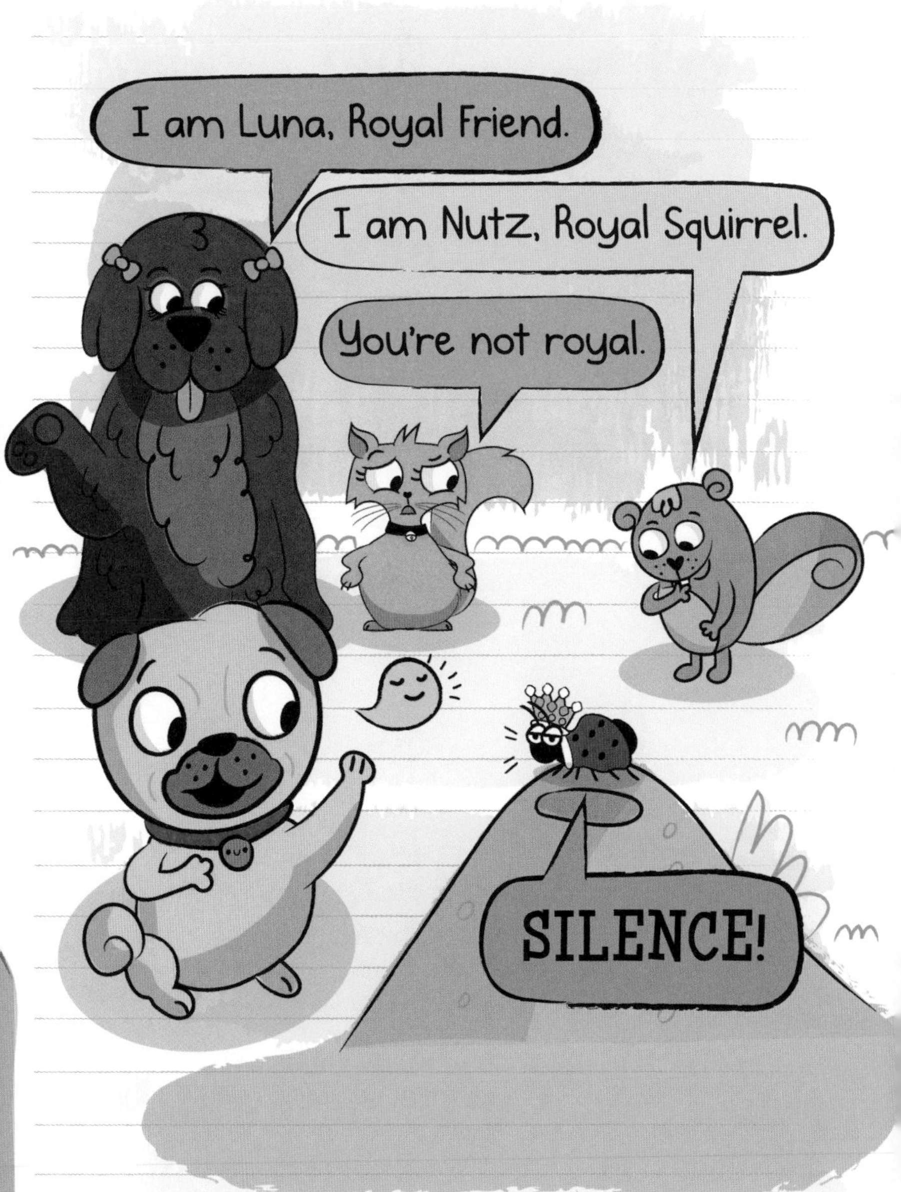
I am Luna, Royal Friend.
I am Nutz, Royal Squirrel.
You're not royal.
SILENCE!

I told her about the parade and how much help Bella needed getting everything done.

Maybe it wasn't the best idea to ask
ants for help, Diary. But Bella couldn't do
it all on her own. What could go wrong?

Chapter 6

LOSING THE CROWN

THURSDAY

Dear Diary,

Turns out when you bring ants home with you, a LOT can go wrong.

After you, My Queen.

The ants couldn't play the ukulele or write Bella's speech. But they said they could make flowers and hang posters.

The ants didn't put up posters, though. They crawled all over the kitchen. They even crawled on Bear!

Maybe this can be OUR forever home.

No way!

They crawled on the washing machine just as Bella's mom was washing Bella's parade shirt.

Everything started going wrong, Diary! Bella's mom used the wrong setting on the washing machine! Bella's shirt shrunk!

Oh no. What have I done?

Maybe it will fit you, Bubby.

Then the ants found my peanut butter!

Cleaning up took a while. But it gave Bella a chance to think.

I've been just like the ants . . . all over the place! The most important thing is to let people know about the parade.

Bella and Jack put up extra posters around town. Meanwhile, I made Bella's crown look extra fancy.

Oh no! I used too much glue! It's stuck!

I should have seen this coming.

Remember how much I hate water, Diary? But I had no choice.

Your royal bath is ready.

Can't blame me for this one.

You're sure this is the only way to get rid of the glue?

I brought the soggy, muddy crown back to Bella.

Oh no! My crown!

I'm so sorry.

I felt terrible, Diary. How could Bella be a queen without a crown?

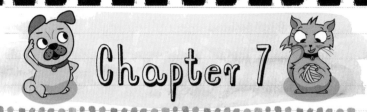

Chapter 7

FIT FOR A QUEEN

FRIDAY

Dear Diary,

Bella was able to make a new crown for the parade. Phew!

You hold the crown while I glue this on, Bub. Thanks!

Bella knew we had been trying to help.

Thanks, royal friends.
Are you ready for the parade?

Yes!

Let's do this!

I picked out the perfect new parade outfit for Bella.

I'm the prince of fashion!

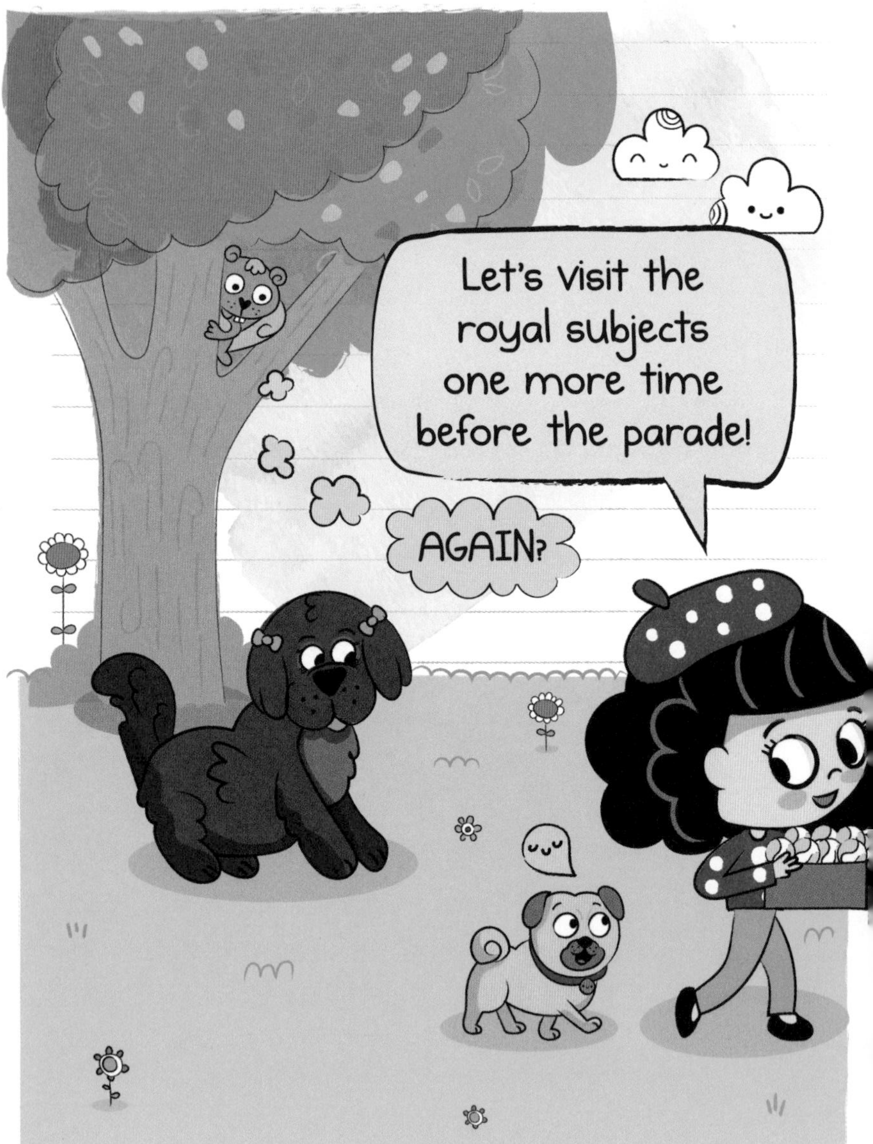
Let's visit the royal subjects one more time before the parade!
AGAIN?

At the shelter, Bella gave out royal hugs and tennis balls. I brought a special surprise for Chester.

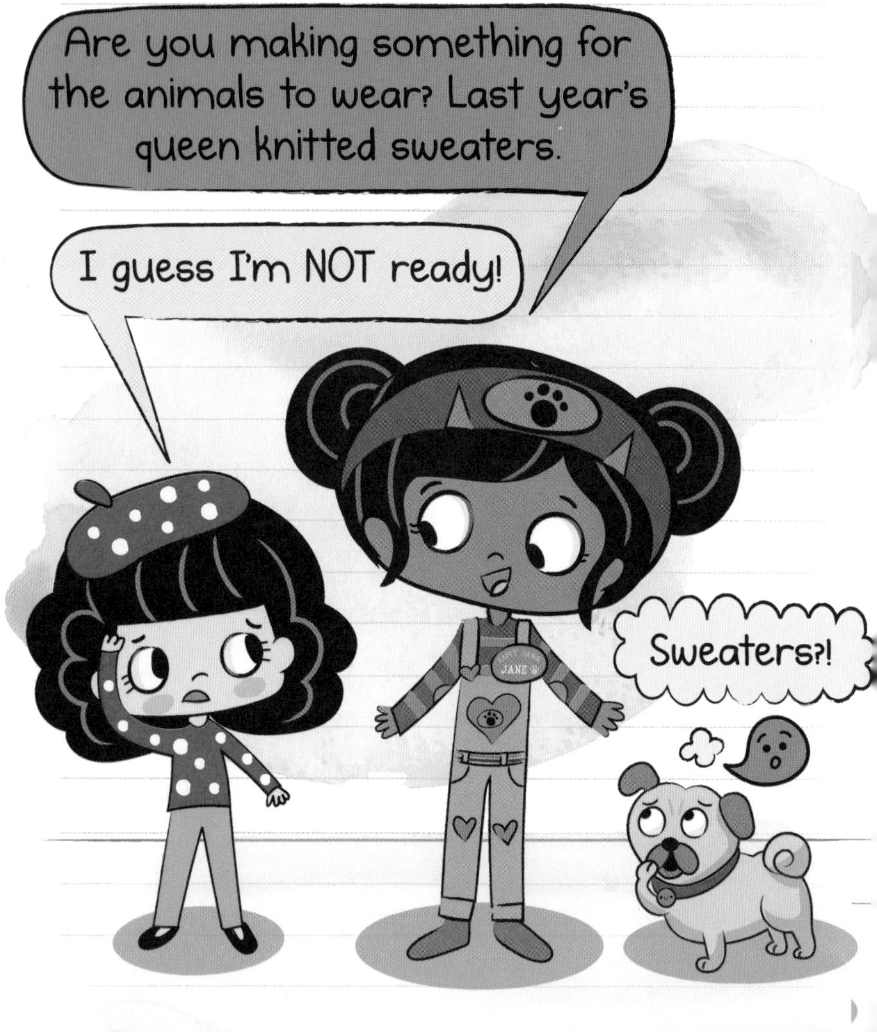
Are you making something for the animals to wear? Last year's queen knitted sweaters.
I guess I'm NOT ready!
JANE
Sweaters?!

After a few more royal hugs, we rushed home. Bella got her mother's knitting basket.

I can't learn to knit by tomorrow.

Yarn! Beautiful yarn!

This seems like a bad idea.

I got untangled and hopped on my skateboard. It was fun to do something I was good at. Luna went next door for a swim. She's a pro!

We all have different talents. I'll be a prince in my own way. And Bella can be a queen in her own way, too.

Just then, Bella got a great idea.

I know what we can make the animals to help them get adopted!

A soggy old crown?

Muddy paw prints?

But the parade is tomorrow! Will we finish in time?

Chapter 8

A ROYAL CELEBRATION

SATURDAY

Dear Diary,

The day of the parade was finally here! Bella wore her crown. I wore mine.

And we brought crowns for every dog and cat at the shelter.

We had stayed up late making them. My muddy paw prints gave Bella the idea. Bella and Jack cut out the patterns.

Nutz added his prints when no one was looking. So did the ants.

Jack and Bella added a dot of glue to hold each crown together.

At the shelter, Bella gave crowns to all the animals. Everyone looked so royal!

Then we got on the parade float.

Bella played the ukulele and sang. The song didn't sound perfect, but it was fun.

Be kind to dogs and cats!
Be kind to rabbits and bats!
Be kind to animals, big and small!
Be kind, be kind to them all!

The crowns made each royal subject look great, especially Chester.

At the end of the parade, Bella made her speech.

... and the shelter helps dogs and cats find families who love them!

Chester even met his forever family!

Thanks for adopting this sweet dog.

Wait until you see your new yard, Chester!

Lots of animals got adopted, Diary.

I couldn't have been queen without you, royal friends!

It turns out Bella made a great queen, Diary. And I was a great royal friend—Prince Bub!

About the Creator

Kyla May♥

Kyla May is an Australian illustrator, writer, and designer. Before creating children's books, Kyla created animation and designed toys. She lives by the beach in Victoria, Australia, with her three daughters, two cats, and three dogs, including her golden retriever puppy, Harlow. The character of Bub was inspired by her daughter's pug, Bear.

HOW MUCH DO YOU KNOW ABOUT
DIARY OF A PUG

Pug the Prince?

 How did I become queen of the animal parade?

 Bella is a queen. What is my royal title?

 What instrument did Bella learn to play? If you could play any instrument, what would it be?

What happened to the first crown Bella made?

 One insect that has a queen is an ant. What is another type of insect with a queen? Reread Chapter 5 to find the answer!

scholastic.com/branches